The Big-Headed People

And Other Stories

D. F. Lewis

The Big-Headed People
by D. F. Lewis

ISBN: 978-1-908125-56-9

Cover Art by David Rix

Publication Date: December 2017

All text copyright 2017 D. F. Lewis

The first half of The Big-Headed People was published in *Marked to Die: A Tribute to Mark Samuels* (Snuggly Books, 2016; edited by Justin Isis)

The Three Ages of D. F. Lewis (1948 -)

1. 1986-2000 – Over 1000 fiction publications in magazines and anthologies, culminating in the Prime Books *Weirdmonger* collection.

2. 2001-2010 – Publishing *Nemonymous* journal of fiction.

3. 2008 to date – Gestalt real-time reviews. (Plus one novel entitled *Nemonymous Night*, a collection, four novellas that were independently published and three originally created multi-authored anthologies.)

Contents

The Big-Headed People

I always knew, physically speaking, I had a big head. My mother complained about the difficult labour she had with me as a result. Later, I sometimes felt I was carrying around a burden, not only because of the head's thoughts with which I needed to deal (as we all do, I presume), but also because of what this conception of a weighty object balanced upon a relatively thin neck was. One of my dinner-party jokes was about needing enough space for both my brains. The only real acknowledgement I made to its size.

But it wasn't exactly a problem. It wasn't *outlandishly* large, and, for most of my life, I never gave it a second thought. Indeed, it later became more in proportion to my portly physique, the neck beneath it soon thickening with middle- and eventually old-age, and the stomach swelling to a size that had more to do with beer than anything else. Or so my wife told me.

I ought to add that I never considered myself to be big-headed in the figurative sense of being arrogant. In fact, most of my life, I suffered from the opposite, as I felt a sense of reticence and diffidence based upon an inferiority complex. I was an only child. Still am, of course.

I first met my big-headed brother, meanwhile, in what I initially considered to be dreams, but as time has gone by, I have begun to consider my so-called real life as a dream or a serial of broken dreams. Whether my actual dreaming when asleep had become my real life outside of sleep did not logically follow on from that, of course. It was a beta situation, still being tested, I told myself.

Some of you will now point to my still-big head and screw your fingers round and round, implying that lots of old people like me confuse dream with real life. Well, I screw my own finger back at you and at your relatively tiny heads. Not that I am implying that the old adage – tiny heads, tiny minds – holds any water!

I shall call this big-headed brother by the name he called himself: Francis, later Frank.

Frank told me that his house was in a place where other big-headed people lived, where, in fact, only big-headed people lived.

In the early days, we merely sat in his living-room, not unlike my own living-room. Comparing heads.

Being brothers, Frank and I had heads of similar size, although the features on our faces were smeared across slightly out of kilter with each other. As if the painter had lost his skill from one portrait to another. Not that we ever agreed which portrait was which!

Over quite a long period, Frank and I got used to each other, not only to the phrenology of our heads but also to the personalities contained within them. He was slightly more confident about life than me, but he did bow to my greater wisdom on many an occasion. However, his confidence gradually took full sway – not a confidence-trick as such, but more a way of enticing my acceptance that he knew a lot about the place where big-headed people lived – and eventually he suggested we ventured outside the house and expanded our horizons by meeting a few of them.

He warned me that our own heads were nothing by which to judge.

"You have seen nothing yet, young Desmond," Frank often said. "There are some very sad people out there."

There is indeed sadness about big heads, I always thought, as they tend to look heavy. But one can never really judge whether other people are depressed simply by the inferred weightiness of their heads. I had always assumed Frank was a happy man, but maybe he wasn't. I now wondered whether or not he thought I was happy. With shared parents, we were probably of similar mentalities, but neither of us could clearly remember those parents.

I nodded at what he said and, soon after that, we ventured out.

I was astonished that the area in which Frank lived was not a city or town. Not even a village, in fact. The reason I had assumed he lived in some built-up area is now beyond me to understand. You see, I cannot recall ever hearing traffic outside or ambulance sirens or anything like that. So when I saw a land stretching into a distance of valleys and hills, I should have accepted it quite equivocally. But I must have looked quite confused, because Frank said: "Desmond, Desmond, surely you knew I lived here."

"Yes, Frank, I knew you lived here, but I did not know you lived *here*." I waved my hand from one end of the warm blue sky to the other.

It was then I spotted the distant tower, indicating perhaps a community.

"Is that where the big-headed people live?"

"They live all over the place."

"Is that a church, then, all on its own?"

"It is not a church as you understand it. But it is a high enough church, however, and its tower radiates a mystical power over us all, without our needing to visit it."

We had already walked quite a distance while talking about this 'church', as if entranced by it. So when I turned to look at Frank's house, it was too late to inspect its nature as an abode, hidden as it now was by a slope of undergrowth. It was then I noticed the first person since leaving that house, almost stumbling upon him, as I did, on the wayside of the rough track where a stile led into a meadow. The man leant against it, as if resting his head, for a while, before resuming his journey. The head was indeed noticeably bigger than Frank's or mine. His face was vaguely doleful, amid otherwise smoothed-out expressionlessness.

"How are you, good sir?" asked Frank confidently.

"Nobbut middling, Frank," he replied lugubriously.

"This is my brother, Desmond, who is visiting the area for the first time."

"Pleased to meet you, Desmond. I've been happy to know your brother for many years." He offered me his hand, with a slowly mooning smile. He had a cotton bud in his left ear.

I took his hand firmly (having been taught by my father from childhood never to offer anyone handshakes like wet fish) and we then exchanged gentlemanly small talk for quite a few minutes, before Frank and I moved on. It was only later I realised that Frank had not actually introduced him properly to me by name.

It was difficult to tell whether or not we were heading in the general direction of the tower, as the contours of the pleasant countryside intervened. And, before long, we met a second person, this time a woman, one with a head slightly bigger even than the previous encounter. She had some sort of upholstered device resting on her shoulder that served to support the weight of her head. I was rather taken aback at how she seemed disabled simply by having to bear this head in the normal course of her life.

Frank did not seem to know her and she only nodded to us in the way complete strangers would nod to each other when passing on a countryside walk, with no real desire to hold a proper conversation. However, I felt tears in my eyes as I turned to Frank and said: "We should have offered our help. She looked as if she was struggling to carry on."

"No, Desmond, there are many people like her, and if we stopped to help everyone we would never get home again. And, indeed, you have seen nothing yet."

And he was right. Around the next corner, we came across a man who was literally laid low, his head so big, it seemed bigger than the rest of him. But that was because his head was the nearest part of him to us, the rest of his body tapering into a ditch. He seemed quite comfortable as what appeared to be yellow mud cushioned his head.

I was perturbed that he had fallen into the ditch, but Frank assured me he was only resting, at a convenient comfortable configuration of land to support the flow of his head and body. I bent down and looked into his eyes.

"He seems to be crying . . ." I said, looking up at Frank. But Frank was looking away as if preoccupied with something else. And before

Frank could respond, the man himself spoke in a kindly half-whisper, half-outspoken singsong:

"I'm not really crying, just thinking of the past. I shall get up in a moment and be on my way."

"Can we help at all?" I asked. "There are two of us here. Each of us under each arm and you'll be up in a trice."

"Where are you from? Where are you off to?" the man asked, as if testing whether we could be trusted. "Are you heading towards the tower?"

I didn't know how to answer, but Frank suddenly became involved:

"One can never reach the tower, however far one travels."

"Speak for yourself, young man." A tone of irony there from the laid-low man, or of cheeky politeness, as Frank was almost as old as I was. "I am travelling there myself and hope to reach it before long. They say it has the highest priests in the land even though the church itself doesn't have the tallest tower. And I have spent my life hoping to receive confession at their hands."

I lowered my head. I didn't want him to see that I was crying, too. If I had been able, I would have given him confession myself there and then. But I did not believe I had the qualification to do so, nor did I believe in what he believed in.

I told him that I would reach the tower and prepare the priests for his arrival. That would be half the battle, at least. And, if the worst happened, and if he didn't reach the tower, then they would know about his pilgrimage towards them and pray for his soul, instead.

When we left him, he was smiling.

I did reach the tower, in the end, having lost Frank along the way. Sadly, it was derelict, with most of the church in ruins, but the tower itself was, with some difficulty, climbable. And indeed I climbed it, negotiating the spiral stairs to the tower's highest point; the sides of the wall were barely wide enough to allow the passage of my head.

I was determined however at least to view eventually, from such a height, the whereabouts of Frank's house, so as to guide my return towards where this dream had begun, if dream it was. Or at least view the nature of his house itself, beyond the dumpty hills.

Some have since asked – what happened next?

Well, I know many thought that my head's width barely by-passing the inner walls of the tower, as I climbed to the top, was some metaphor for the act of birth, the difficulty which my mother had originally suffered in bearing down on me. But I had shrugged my shoulders each side of my increasingly heavy head, as at birth I was travelling towards the top of something not the bottom.

Once back on the ground, would I travel back, as I had expected, to Frank's so-called house – perhaps, along the way, meeting again the poor souls I had met when walking with Frank to the tower? But now, with Frank gone, I had a sudden urge to travel onward, beyond the tower, over untrodden ground. It seemed years since I had arrived at the tower, but it must have been only about an hour before. The structure had given me none of the religion in which I had once assumed its building materials were steeped. A mis-consecration, perhaps, rather than a formal de-consecration.

It was abruptly at that point when I saw the signs of an urban area in the onward distance. How had I missed that from when I was at the top of the tower? And then I remembered I had, once up there, looked only backward at where I thought Frank's house would be . . . a house that was, I recall, some sort of mirage of the biggest head of them all, the reality of which I could now only doubt.

What would I find in such a city, if city it was that I had spotted? I saw what I took to be the low-slung bungalows of its suburbs, and the slightly taller buildings beyond them. I could not make out any details in what had become a mist, but I suddenly started thinking, with some sad dread, about what size heads its citizen had to bear, judging by how big the people had already become the further I had walked from Frank's house. But, then again, I could easily imagine city folk, as opposed to country folk, enjoying smaller heads, small enough in fact as to match the heads of some of the so-called freaks in Tod Browning's famous film, freaks if only in name.

Without further ado, with the darkening time overdue, I set forth towards what I can only describe as the fuzzy margins of a new personal adventure. And I soon found myself in a form of no man's land where countryside meets city. A run-down area, where what I had mistaken for bungalows were in fact shanties. I could sense no presence of people, but I soon reached what seemed to be a shopping precinct, shop-fronts too badly-lit to disperse the increasing gloom, and in one I could vaguely see, for sale, some of those head harnesses that I had earlier seen the woman on the country path wearing, except here were available sizes of harness far in excess of the one her head had needed. Such a sight brought back the earlier sadness, a deep-seated anxiety about myself and the fate of Frank, someone who, in hindsight, I wrote off too glibly, never explaining why he failed to accompany me the whole way to the tower, a memory in itself even now still fading . . . as I felt the contours of my own head with a similar anxiety as I saw its blurred reflection in the harness display window . . .

My attention was abruptly drawn to another storefront. It was as if someone or something had moved in the shadows, automatically bringing my whole body around in that direction. The previously unnoticed items of lighting – old-fashioned street furnishings with many of them slightly leaning over – flickered into being, and I saw what I thought were robots or tin dolls or metallic mannequins or of some such kind behind a shop window, half-sized or child-sized like some of the human beings I remembered from the aforementioned cinema film whose title I have now forgotten. Some of them in the window had encrusted rust at their groins. Signs of incontinence, I thought, a thought which reminded me that I needed to relieve myself, a fact that had crept up on me before reaching my conscious mind. A whole day where I seem to have forgotten such a natural human requirement or forgotten where and how often I had already fulfilled it.

At least, the sight of the metal heads, glinting in a sudden reappearance of a very low sun – heads as of average size when compared to their bodies – was a relief in quite a different way, inexplicably lifting my anxiety. And it was at that point I swivelled, for just an intended moment, back towards the path along which I had arrived and made out in the distance the derelict tower itself, with a big cross brightly lit upon it.

What happened between then and now is told, I'm told, in detail elsewhere by another source, someone I do not know, and anyone I do not know is automatically undependable. My own mind is clear, though, that I can remember nothing about how I found myself sitting in a courtroom, one of plain varnished wood panels and a light source that was eked out by high windows just below the ceiling level, a ceiling that was a naïve painting of two big-headed angels stretching out a single finger to each other, tantalisingly not yet touching.

How long I had been sitting in what I thought must be the courtroom's dock, I cannot tell you, but as soon as I was conscious of my position, a door opened and a man whom I took to be a court official entered with a tape measure around his neck. He was a jobsworth, I could already tell, an inscrutable retired soldier, I guessed, as he proceeded to measure the contours of my head, without a word passing between us. His own head, I estimated, was more than just slightly bigger than mine. His breath rancid.

Already I had noticed the wooden benches around the edges of the courtroom, high, medium and low, to house the seating, I assumed, of the judges, jury and public watchers. And I was not wrong.

The five judges eventually trooped in from the judicial vestry, heads at least as big as to match that of the woman with a harness I had met earlier. Their own harnesses were a crafty contraption that combined white bony-woollen wigs with struts. They sat sternly, and somewhat precariously, in the high bench.

The jury had already been sworn in . . .

Hey, why was I in the dock at all, I suddenly thought to ask. And why was I taking all of this ritual procedure for granted? I had done nothing wrong. But then I noticed that the jury with variously-sized heads, mostly bigger than mine, one or two smaller, and one of them dawningly recognisable to me, being very small indeed; it was surely a randomly chosen group of (I counted) thirteen that – I saw even more suddenly at that point! – included my brother Frank and my wife whom I shall leave nameless. They both averted their eyes as if in a signal not to divulge their presence. They were obviously there to help my cause. But how had they managed to pull the wool over the eyes of the judges?

It was at that point the middle Judge of the five suddenly started speaking with a voice that was modulated to sound boring and structured to feel ungrammatical:

"You in the dock, you are accused of head slimming, a crime forbidden in this city, slimming being OK when done with the rest of the body, a healthy practice, but offering your services to our citizens to slim their heads instead is a heinous crime and we have a film taken showing you practising this operation. We shall show that film, despite its nature of horror, should we need to do so, and the jury and the public witnesses here have been warned that they may be made unwell by seeing it, so it is in your obvious interest to bleed guilty at this stage. How do you bleed?"

I must have looked confused, but the inscrutable official forced me to my feet, and I uttered the words: "Not guilty."

"Not guilty, my lord," the official prompted, forcing an unknown orange book into my hand. He had a voice after all.

"Not guilty, my lord," I said, this time trying to lend more certainty to my words.

Those on the public bench brayed, their heads moving from side to side like giant barrage balloons.

Immediately, blinds came down on the windows, as if by remote control, and a screen rose from the floor, somehow visible to the whole room, all the possible perspectives of any scenario being best described in words. Better than any image, moving or not.

The interior of the operation room was at first hardly discernible. But gradually the camera focused on a trestle-table and, then, the chintzy décor of the walls came into slightly softer focus, with gilt-framed big-headed portrait paintings upon gaudy wallpaper. Lying on the table was a human shape swaddled, from the neck down, in what looked to be animal hide, his or her head seeming to be as big as some of the biggest heads known to populate the city. Gradually, the lower face could be seen to have a beard, not a shadow on the chin. A moustache, too, not a slug crawling above the top lip. The look in his eyes was baleful, but full of the ability to pay for whatever service was to be given to him. The nose, ears, eyes and mouth were out of scale to the rest of the head. It had never been questioned, before this lying camera came into play, whether big-headed people just possessed over-sized skulls, but skulls with an average-sized head's average-sized appendages otherwise. If this lying example was to be believed, then the chances were that big-headed people in general had heads with appendages actually in correct scale to the size of their heads, evidence that this was therefore a false image on the screen. So if that was false, the rest was probably false, too. But before further thought could be given to this contention, there was an abrupt turn of the camera towards one of this city's child-sized robots, evidently an ornament on the room's old-fashioned sideboard, but – suddenly clearer – it was not an ornament at all, as it began to climb from its plinth in a slow, measured way. It had taken with it a sort of cutting implement with a jagged edge, much larger than a creature of this size would normally be able to handle. There were sound effects, too, with the robot's metal squeaking and grinding, its evidently rusty joints de-crusting as it moved after such a long period standing where it had been standing. Brown smears in its wake. An intention of its own, rather than anyone controlling it? A sense that its leakings are caused by the constriction of some foreign prostate. And as these thoughts pass through the camera, it approaches the trestle table and close-ups are given of the blade entering the skin behind one of the ears, but obviously some other instrument is required for the bone that has thus been revealed. Another figure has joined the 'robot', a shadowy, hooded human figure it seems, emerged from one of the chintzy walls, as it were, evidently claimed to be the accused himself, although others have counter-claimed that the 'patient' looks like the accused, if with a bigger head! The hooded figure has started sawing at the bone wherever the robot has revealed such bone with its slicing, from eye socket to eye socket, and at the back where the hair, just above an undrained sebaceous cyst, gets in the way of a clean operation. But gradually, and surprisingly, the bone is pared back, piecemeal, like preparing the ground for an inner quilt of skullbone, as if there is a head within a head, which it was known there couldn't possibly be. Two brains, maybe, but not two heads, that apparent suggestion of two brains being a sort of sick joke by the devious camera as it made things clearer with each serration and incision. No, it was a genuine paring back, not the revelation of a smaller head within the original head. Most would find this an ordeal to watch, as the film itself made clear by visually expunging the most gruesome moments, the film itself censoring itself as part of the censored picture it was showing, but the gory implications of what had been censored were also being shown subliminally . . .

I remember the image on the courtroom screen suddenly vanishing to a dot, like those old-fashioned TVs that I and my parents once watched in the 1950s, with their falling asleep every night in front of the tiny screen, their eyelids drooping, swollen and ripe for plucking, I always thought. What a waste of a life the coming of the TV caused that generation who had been social beasts before then. Much like the internet today for newer generations, not that I really remembered everything about my past before visiting my elusive, perhaps essentially non-existent, brother in his dumpty house all that time ago. It was only then I realised that the film had only been in black and white, and thanks to the tower at least for that!

I now found myself in a Spartan cell, with very little light. The officious courtroom man had left me here, and I inferred I had been found guilty. I had been here years, perhaps, and over such a lengthy time, one thinks.

And what I thought was that I had been found guilty by ten to three jurors, the job of the five judges merely being to allow a majority verdict, and nothing else. I laughed at the pomp of their contraptive wigs. And their laws about head slimming.

Having now finally dealt with the thoughts, I suddenly remembered for the first time that my mother, the one who had originally had the task of bearing my head, had been on the jury, too. And my father was there, of course, someone whom now I abruptly realised was disguised as my brother, a brother I had never had. And, of course, my dear small-headed wife. Thank goodness, she and I were due to leave two good children behind when we had finally gone. With average-sized heads, of course.

But thoughts have to end eventually. Thoughts can make the head bigger and bigger until it can get no bigger. The squeaking and grinding are approaching now from beyond the cell door. Not just one but many.

But I still had the orange book in my hand.

A Halo of Drizzle Around
an Orange Street Lamp

Alma's ambition was to hold a picnic at night. She knew, of course, that there were many occasions when people held beach parties that entailed picnics and that could last past the setting of the sun or even start after it had set. But that was not a picnic proper, she was sure. She also knew of the expression 'maroon-party' – a real expression – something that signified a long-term picnic, often stretching for days and days on end. That would have entailed, no doubt, a series of night-time picnics as part of such a marathon picnic known as a maroon-party. No, none of those pseudo-picnics were for Alma; they were not picnics proper at all.

For Alma, a picnic was an occasion with a table-cloth or a picnic-dedicated chequered sheet spread over a meadow – usually beneath durable sunshine – and laid with fine-china crockery and crystal wine-glasses, filled by thermos flasks of hot beverage at the basest or bottles of vintage wine at the highest, accompanied by neatly manicured cucumber sandwiches brought to the picnic in wicker hampers. And other comestibles of similar ilk. Even pork-pies despite the heat – even melon mivvis and choc-ices kept in a cool-bag. A motley collection of provender besieged by happy children flickering with smiles, administered by family hierarchies from great grandparents downward – and the sound of laughter and easy gurgling and the mischievously loud chomping of teeth. And light repartee as well as political discussion among the grown-ups.

"Why on Earth, Alma, do you want us to have a proper picnic at night time?"

Her husband looked bemused having heard a potted history of her future plans.

"Well, I had a dream about a proper picnic at night time. It just seemed fun. And something to write about in the journal section in the Family Bible for our little ones' little ones to read about for posterity. For when things are all technological and nobody has proper picnics at all. Perhaps they will at least relive our night time picnic . . . you know, to remember us, to remember *me*."

"Perhaps, since you were dreaming about at it *at* night time, Alma, it only seemed to be at night time that the picnic was taking place."

She shrugged her shoulders. She was determined that the whole current family would participate in a night time occasion, short enough to be a proper picnic and not anything else: say, between 2 and 3 in the small hours.

"The little ones shouldn't be allowed to stay up that late, and how on earth are we going to illuminate the whole damn thing, Alma?"

"We can hold it on the recreation ground as far away from the road for the street lamps not to impinge too much but with them near enough so as to see what we are doing. Hopefully a moon, too."

"Yes, it would be very awkward with torches. I can't believe we're even discussing this."

The day of the picnic arrived. Or should we say the night of the picnic was imminently due to be upon them. Alma was busy, that afternoon, preparing all those comestibles and beverages that she had described to her husband many weeks before. They had left it until June, so as to take advantage of more clement weather. Not that the weather seemed to matter so much for a night time occasion. Or perhaps, thinking about it, it mattered even more. But rain is rain whether it's in daylight or darkness, and the question is: which is more miserable, light rain or dark rain? (The double meaning of 'light' was intended. It always seems heavier and wetter and more dismal when you can't see it clearly.)

It certainly wasn't raining at all when the family set out to the recreation ground, carrying hampers and contraptions of comfort. And the forecast was for a clear night with the promise of a bright full moon as the ghost of a picnicking sun. (Some may say a *panicking* sun in today's change of weather patterns caused by global warming, however.)

All the family's little ones had been given permission to stay up late by their respective parents. Everyone knew that Aunt Alma or Grandma Alma or Great Grandma Alma, as she was variously called, was a batty old bat, even if mostly loveable, most of the time. She just needed indulging just this once so that she could translate such an eccentricity of a night time picnic – as a real-time fact of her diminishing life – into the Family Bible's remaining blank fly-leaves: translated by or into the form of her characteristic spidery handwriting.

They used a white sheet to spread over the grass. The promised moon arrived, too. Even so, the little ones were strangely muted. Not because they were tired; they had changed their sleeping patterns to suit the unusual waking hours entailed by this dyschronological event. No, the case was that they seemed inhibited by the darkness itself – a darkness only marginally dispersed by the orange street-lighting – and they seemed also eager to stay close to the edges of the spread sheet, upon which the various items of picnicking were now being placed . . . rather than charging back and forth with childish whoops and hoops. Alma and her husband (for the record, her third husband) were officiating from two garden chairs erected at the north end of the sheet. She shivered as a breeze ruffled her hat's feathers.

But not only a breeze, but other auguries of ill. The moon was indeed a ghost, but now not the sun's ghost, but its own ghost. And the orange street lamps became more like splats than spots.

I could go to the Family Bible itself – a record that I shall call a primary source from a historical point of view – to seek out the nature of later events. That would make for a much longer story. But I haven't yet checked to see if there is anything written there about Alma's picnic at all, even if it turns out to be merely couched by indecipherable spidery writing that possibly disowns any posterity whatsoever.

Suffice to tell you that I am depending on hearsay and rumour when I mention that the dark shapes and silhouettes of street-housing beyond the orange lamps were being hidden themselves by larger shapes and silhouettes that were not items of housing at all – shapes and silhouettes that eventually concealed signs of the local council's civic lighting utilities that had been placed there in better days for health and safety.

Later, there were whoops and hoops from night's true picnickers – the now invisible hungry shapes – as they approached to picnic upon Alma's family of muted panickers. And one marooned street lamp was left with a visible halo of drizzle. Till even that one went out. Or left.

Thoughts and Themes

There was only one way the circus could reach the recreation ground – via the 1950s council estate with relatively narrow roads. Real animals were no longer permitted to perform in circuses but, in the old days, they used to poke their bald or shaggy heads through the bars of the trundling cages and roar or bleat or bark or crow at the curious bystanders on the grass-edged pavements. Today, only clowns stared out with painted-on smiles beneath their unsuitable frowns. The odd acrobat, too.

John was not on the pavement himself; he was inside the house looking through his front room window. He must have got things wrong. The slow-moving cages from where he was standing seemed full of animals. Then, squeezing his eyes, they turned back into clowns – trundling past carefully to avoid the water hydrants and street lighting. In the old days, the lamp-posts would have been turned off by this time of the night, John remembered. If cars were parked in the road, they needed side-lights till the morning.

It was becoming chilly as the last circus vehicle ground past with a spluttering exhaust. How the circus people managed to transport the Big Top and all its poles around these roads was quite beyond him. In the old days, it seemed that the whole affair appeared as if by magic over one night on the recreation ground without anyone noticing. These days, everyone seemed to make a song and dance about everything – especially kids with things on their ears. And people seemed awake at all hours as if time was now non-stop, he thought.

He turned to the front room fire. In the old days, he needed good kindling to get it roaring. Now, it was just a single flick of a switch that was needed – but he could hardly afford the bills. Nor did he really understand how to set the timer.

Morning came. John was in bed. I had taken over from him at the front room window – expecting it to be chillier than it actually was. The storage heater was working better today, I could tell. I laughed to myself as I saw John's carefully piled kindling in a scuttle near a disused companion-set. He still kept the kindling going in case the storage heater ceased working, but I don't reckon he had thought about whether the chimney needed cleaning after all these years of disuse. Kindling seemed to be the theme of the night just departed. That and clowns' frowns. There were often themes and thoughts that John left for me after he had gone to bed. As if he expected me to carry them on in some renewed shift of life and of life's thinking.

I knew as if instinctively that a circus procession had passed the house during the night, not least of all because of the themes and thoughts that John had left for me. Well, not so much instinct as also discerning the piles of animal droppings in the gutter that kids were now kicking around on the way to school. And the red-bobbled hat that probably fell off one of the clown's heads during a prolonged frown. And a loose tent-pole section leaning against a lamp-post like a midget vaulter's cast-off. Or a trapeze-artist's missing hand-hold. Or a ring-master's ludicrously large baton.

If John were still awake he would have gone straight out there – kids or not – to retrieve that pole for later snapping into further kindling. And darted straight back before he reached it, no doubt!

When John got up, ready for his shift, I suggested we both went to the recreation ground and buy a ticket for the circus. He frowned, knowing that neither of us were gadabouts and we wouldn't bother going out at all, when push came to shove. We were homebirds, first and foremost. Underpinners of life's themes or thoughts, second. Trial experimenters of the outside world, third and rarely. Normal human beings, last and never.

Still, we weren't stick-in-the-muds. We had clown costumes as well as many other devices in-house already and we could muster up our own circus at the slightest swing of a ringmaster's metaphorical baton. Many a day after that, when our shifts overlapped we would sit in opposite armchairs frowning at each other like off-duty clowns. Breaking glances till one of us retired for the night or the rest of the day. Kindling for needed dreams, perhaps.

Themes and thoughts never do reach a conclusion. It was my turn to stand watch at the front room window tonight. The gathering shadows couldn't be the kids. Kids needed sleep more than most once they had slotted their screens away where screens were kept. Made their mobiles immobile. Left their dreams beneath the deep unbroken sleep of the innocent. No, the shadows that kept siege upon our house were not kids; these shadows had fire frowns glimmering: at one moment like eyes, the next as forlorn bobbled headgear too large to keep from slipping down over their faces, but finally disguised as lamp-post embers or a parked car's side-light glances. None of the houses on the estate had garages or drives. I couldn't call John awake as neither of us dared do this to the other for fear of what we might conjure up, conjure up or kindle. Worse than anything was a wasted or duplicated shift.

I kept the window open upon the seemingly endless night, so as to hear the expelled breath of a distant tent toppling. Or to stop me hearing that of a lung giving out, more like. A large tent as far away as the recreation ground or a small one closer to home sounded much the same. An odd acrobat of the mind. Send in the frowns. Then send them back. A relentless rhythm of sadness and forgotten joy. Thoughts and themes in storage perhaps forever.

Origami Shadows

Terry – his wife knew – had a new hobby. There was an unaccustomed silence about things. He was normally very busy-looking, noisily dodging from garden to shed to upstairs eaves-cupboards merely for show, the rest of the time getting in her way and making 'suggestions'. Sometimes she imagined Bill and Ben jumping in and out of their flowerpots each time he entered and exited the garden in a frenzy of non-activity. She laughed.

He couldn't sit still with a book or the TV, and he hated the new-fangled internet. He liked hard copies of everything. Even, his wife thought, of her! A stationary waxwork model with lipsticked mouth in the lounge, as long as the housework and the cooking still got done by some miracle of mysterious serendipity. Retirement had never really suited him. She hoped he might get into music because, as a boy, he told her, he had been made to learn the piano. But all his life he couldn't decide what form of music he liked, so he decided he disliked all music, just a waste of time, nothing constructive about it, although deep down he'd probably love *all* music if he gave it a chance and allowed it to jump that last hurdle-block of acceptance by his otherwise highly musical brain.

Then, that day of which is spoken, she saw Terry . . . nowhere. He seemed too quiet even to be present and correct in the house at all, although she instinctively knew he was there somewhere: his presence was in every corner, but not the corner she happened to be looking at when he happened to be *in* that corner: a relatively small house, so it should not have been difficult to find him.

This story knew where he was, all the time, but it was not letting on about it; it never liked truth being misrepresented as fiction and being called a story; that would have meant it was being severely misjudged or maligned by whoever was writing it. The story was therefore sulking. Sulking and moping in another corner from where Terry was ensconced – sure in its own heart that reality was its gift to the world not make-believe.

There must come a time, however, when all cards should be laid on the table; otherwise madness or, worse, unreality and untruth would begin to prevail. Terry's wife indeed was becoming frantic . . . but she had not been brought into the story just to be cruel to her (had she?) or to make her go frantic with worry. She'd be ringing the police next and that unintended development would surely need addressing sooner or later by the Powers of Plot, so-called.

So, there was Terry – not in the garden shed as she had assumed – not even in the toilet or crouched within an eaves cupboard – but in the lounge all the time: seated on the couch: the large jigsaw-layout board on his lap: and oblongs and squares of flimsy-to-stiff coloured card or paper scattered like a mapmaker's confused dream . . .

"Oh, there you are," he said, as he spotted his wife in the doorway. "Where have you been?" She was wearing well for her age, he noticed. Better than him, he feared.

He seemed to peer through the window into the garden or into the corner near the window as if appealing to some force to right all wrongs in the world as he saw them. Not going to work anymore allowed for such things to cross his mind, even if it wasn't quite in those words or in those terms. It was more a hovering sense or sensibility of mixed-up, if ever-slowly clarifying, emotions – rather than anything he could put his finger on about which to articulate.

"I could have asked the same thing," she snapped back. "Have you been out without telling me?" But in her heart of hearts she had always known that he hadn't gone out. The house was Terry. The house without Terry was quite a different house. Not that it wasn't the Terry house much these days, as he hardly ever went out. So where had he been if he hadn't left the house?

"Been here the whole time. Started origami. Found a book about it in the eaves cupboard. It looked just up my street."

"Where did you get those?" She nodded at the pieces of card.

"Found them there, too. Can't remember ever having seen them before."

She tried to visualise how dark it was in their eaves cupboards. And how cluttered.

"Did you use the torch?"

"Couldn't find it?"

"You couldn't find the torch but *could* find the origami book!" she said with much surprised puzzlement.

The Terry House seemed to expel a short sharp sigh as if it was getting rid of some emotion in an oriental or mystical way that it had been taught long before Terry and his wife lived there. Before it was the Terry House itself. When it was somebody else's house by name. Somebody more mystical than Terry and his wife. Or simply more oriental.

Both heard the sigh. Or at least sensed it with some other sense than hearing. And both remained silent. Nonplussed.

They had lived here for 15 years, ever since Terry had been made redundant. As she watched, he was folding a piece of light card – pastel-shaded between two different colours the exact nature of which she couldn't be sure – and eventually she saw it forming piecemeal, under his clumsy fingers, into the shape of a . . . strange animal she couldn't quite recognise, possibly a hybrid of a giraffe and a swan.

The story was at cross-purposes with itself; and truth was coming in a poor second to falsehood. The origin of the shape was slowly pre-dating the shape itself under Terry's gauche manipulation of it. The room filled with black shadows as if the eaves cupboard had walked downstairs and become the lounge, while still retaining the size of the lounge. The eaves cupboard perhaps was now a miniature form of the lounge under the roof upstairs. Nobody could be sure. The origami model was playing its own shadow game it seemed, casting silhouettes on the lounge's now roof-sided internal slope, silhouettes that – by means of the various angles or configurations in which the shadows were being thrown then focussed – became recognisable creatures: hybrids of nothing but themselves: a pure-bred elephant, then a fox, followed by a bear, a dog, a cat, a lizard . . . Each in turn pranced to unheard music, then bowed, before the next creature appeared. Only the lizard slithered without prancing. And *its* music was not even unheard.

The story missed a beat. It was sad. It never knew it could create such utter truth from such utter fantasy. It seemed a world away now. Terry was still on the couch and his wife sat next to him – and they were hugging and kissing each other. The lounge was not quite the same as it had ever been before: it still had some of the clutter from the eaves cupboard, but the TV set was back in the corner. The screen empty. The central-heating radiator was also back and the light fitment re-fixed in the ceiling rose. But one of the walls was still a roof-slope rather than the upright brick version that it should have been. And old suitcases that the couple had not seen for donkey's years were piled like a soft-luggage Stonehenge near the exit doorway to the kitchen.

The jigsaw board was tilted against the side of the couch, its origami materials scattered across an unrecognisable carpet. They always say (don't they?) that the last item in any room to rectify itself back into reality is its carpet. Vaguely lizard designs in a boring beige. Designs ever-slowly becoming more geometrical than anything recognisable as lizards. Oriental by origin. Ancient or modern, art deco or pre-Raphaelite, it was impossible to judge. Some antiques often looked more modern than modern things, assuming that the wear and tear hadn't given the game away. Wear and tear. A nasty symptom of origami. Impetigo was another nasty disease, one that Terry had suffered as a small child. Had to be fed by his mother through a straw poked between his cracked and stuck lips. Each card not now delicately pastel-shaded, but stained with the black shadows that each had once proudly given off when shaped up into the shapes they always were before they became mere sheets of card.

Eventually, however, all returned to normal. But Terry and his wife couldn't part their lips. There's nothing more to know about it all.

But maybe the story knew something more. Or the house did.

A story about a story. And a barely discernible run along the keys from a new old piano in the corner.

The Soft Tread

Jill's father used to call it 'age at the edge'. That part of your life when you are not old enough to think yourself an old person, but old enough to have worrying fears that others probably saw you as an old person, fears that you put to the back of the mind. Call it denial, call it whatever you like. When I first met Jill, my way of dealing with any fears or anxieties that impinge on people like us at the edge of age was to see them as a changeable 'weather' front of thoughts and preoccupations. Something you took for granted.

God can control the real weather so why can't we be Gods of our own thought-weather, Jill once asked me. I sensed she was humouring me. Or ridiculing me?

Jill was a lady of – what shall I say? – mature years with less spring in her step than she seemed to have in the old family films she often showed me. In her heyday, I gradually learnt, from these films and the piecemeal information she fed me, that she had five children, six cats, her old father in the converted loft and a husband – and they all lived in a large house that she and her husband together called 'The Mill on the Molehill'. Not an affectionate pet name for their marital abode, it seemed, but a sort of 'compromise' name, she told me. Its address was 89 Old Heath Row, I later discovered. Why that specific detail, even to the exact number on its front door, was relevant for me to know has since faded from my memory.

Anyway, I suspect it wasn't such a large house as she made out. It certainly didn't appear in any of the films because they seemed to be taken from the house out towards the garden. Quite a small garden, in fact. Huge landing and taking-off of aeroplanes did, however, feature regularly. Or at least the huge shadows that they cast upon the playing children of whom the films were mostly taken. Jill herself only appeared a couple of times when I noticed that disguised spring in her step, despite not a sign of spring in her face. Never saw her husband in them, though. And only one cat at a time that all looked identical to each other.

I questioned the house's 'Mill on the Molehill' name with my eyebrows the first time she mentioned it to me.

"Oh, my husband always made mountains out of molehills . . . even when he was younger. I often said that to him. I suppose I shouldn't have. Equally, he often said I put him *through* the mill. You know the expression. As if I ground him down. But that was all in his head. But I *did* put him through the mill, he would repeat. What mill? I asked. The mill of life, he'd say and then sigh."

And she sighed as she said this to me. As if she now admitted she'd put him through the so-called mill after all.

She had some lovely turns of phrase, did Jill. Lovely, in the sense of the words she used, but unkindly meant otherwise. Meaningful but spiteful. Pity I can't recall all her pet sayings. Oh, there's one that sticks in my mind. One of the more thoughtful ones. She said you could always tell what sort of person was coming by the sound of their tread.

"How often do you hear people coming before you see them?" I asked quizzically.

"Oh, you'd be surprised. Like someone coming along the hall."

"But if they're in your hall you should already know who they are."

"Tom, stop being so literal. You know what I mean. If you had two possible people around and one of them was coming along the hall towards where you're sitting in the sitting-room, you can tell a lot from whether it is a hard tread or a soft tread."

"So it's not exactly a method of judging the nature of a stranger approaching. Like telling whether he's old or young . . . or coming with bad or good intent?"

"Oh, you can tell a lot from a tread. Better even than examining the palms of their hands or the iris in one of their eyes."

I laughed. "The iris of the right or left eye?"
She frowned, knowing I was humouring her. Even
ridiculing her. "The tread of a left or right foot?"
I continued to dig an even deeper hole for myself
with my questions. I was now literally spluttering
with laughter. Hardly able to get my words out
now, but I continued: "Can one foot have a hard
tread and the other foot of the same person a soft
one? Or can you tread only with one foot leaving
the other up in the air. Or I suppose that's not
treading but limping . . ."

I was now curled up laughing on the floor.

After a minute's silence, while I tried to stifle
my laughter, curling up even more tightly into a
ball, she announced: "You look like one of my
old cats when I had given up stroking it. When I
was stroking it, however, it would stretch out just
waiting for a bout of tickling and then followed by
gentle stroking. Opening itself up to me without
fear. But then when I had finished it would curl
into a ball, just like you. Like a black rose."

I imagined the silky tread of a black cat drifting
along the hall. I imagined Jill's first husband
himself curling up into a ball when he heard a
large aeroplane brushing their house's rooftop.
That's the sort of thing he would have done, based
on the picture I had been given of him by Jill.
It was probably only a bird not a plane at all. A
molehill not a mountain . . .

I imagined her children, too, curling up into their own balls to stifle things they wanted to say or to ask for or to complain about . . . or to stifle hearing what others wanted to say or to ask for or to complain about to them.

I imagined her first husband again – starting up in his sleep as he heard, from beyond his dreams, her soft springing tread as it came along past the banister's top newel post towards the bedroom.

Then curling up under the covers as if he didn't exist at all.

"Tom! Get up from the floor!" she shouted, breaking my reverie of imaginations.

Dutifully, I did. Arms outstretched like an aeroplane slowly taking off.

My laughing finally stifled. We silently stared into each other's gently whirling eyes, blurred by tears. At least *my* tears.

"How many of you actually lived at 89 Old Heath Row?" I finally managed to ask.

Jill just smiled. And, hand in hand, we dragged our aging limbs upstairs.

Later there would always follow a noise like a large stone slowly revolving on top of another stone. Then silence. Then again that noise. Time and time again. Followed by silence.

We'd play guessing games between the edges of each period of silence. She was Jill, and I was Tom. Never any different.

There was never complete silence, however, due to the soft tread of ghosts coming along the landing. Or the odd suspicion of digging noises from the loft.

We often believed that we had never heard the noise of heavy stones grating in the first place. Or that we would never hear them again. Just Heaven's own weather front.

www.ingramcontent.com/pod-product-compliance
Lightning Source LLC
Chambersburg PA
CBHW032045180726
48284CB00008B/2758